For Charlotte,

Your ability to see the best in all people and circumstances inspires me. Thank you.

Life On
Pandemic Ave

When the pandemic began, things changed for our neighborhood.

Life looks very different right now, but this difference can be an opportunity for creativity. Let's take a look to see how each neighbor is doing.

This is Charlotte, who lives in the first house. She has been at home attending virtual school for a while now, and each day she misses her classmates more and more.

Since she hasn't been able to see her friends in person, she gathers her stuffed animals and pretends they are her classmates.

In the second house, Jayden is reading a book to himself. He is concerned because his grandmother is in the hospital, and he can't see her right now.

To feel close to her, he opens the same story that she reads to him when they are together. He can hear her voice in his mind as he reads, and it comforts him.

James lives in the next house, but he isn't home right now. Today is the first time he's been out in public in quite a while. He is with his mother at the grocery store, where he loves to pretend that he is on an adventure to collect treasured foods.

While on this quest, he decides that the mask he is wearing is a new protective part of his adventure suit. Now he is able to collect the treasured foods while staying safe!

Violet lives in the last house. Each day she plays inside with her sister, but is concerned about Mr. Winston, the elderly man who lives across the street by himself.

She wants him to know that people care about him, and that he is not truly alone. She delivers a letter that says, "Peek out the door at 3pm, so that I can wave to you from my window."

As 3pm arrives, his face and heart beam as
she smiles and waves from her window.

Although circumstances can be hard, in different ways,
we all do the very best we can.

About the Author

Ryan Markley is an aspiring graphic designer. Who she will become is yet to be determined, but in the meantime, she lives to be creative and kind.

Reflection Questions:

1. What has been most challenging for you during the pandemic?

2. Have you noticed any "silver linings" during this time?

3. In what ways have you seen others be creative and kind?

4. How have you tried to be creative and kind?

Memories

Pictures

Made in the USA
Middletown, DE
13 October 2021